© 2008 Dami International srl, Milano-Firenze

This 2009 edition published by Sandy Creek
by arrangement with Dami International srl.

Sandy Creek
122 Fifth Avenue
New York, N.Y. 10011

ISBN - 13: 978 - 1 - 4351 - 1156 - 1

Printed and bound in China

1 3 5 7 9 10 8 6 4 2

from an idea by ANDREA DAMI

Illustrations by Marco Campanella
Text by Anna Casalis
Design by Stefania Pavin

TIP THE MOUSE
DOESN'T WANT TO BEHAVE

Illustrated by

Marco Campanella

SANDY CREEK

Tip is normally a good little mouse, but today he woke up in a very cranky mood.

"Get dressed, Tip," says his mother after breakfast. "Put your shirt on so you will be warm when we go out for a walk."

"I don't want to! I like this T-shirt!" says Tip.

"Well, you will just be chilly then," says his mother. "Before we go, please put your toys away."

"I didn't make the mess, Teddy Bear did! Anyway, I like my toys this way, I can find them better," replies Tip.

Let's go

"Mom, will you buy me a toy?" Tip asks at the store. "I would buy one if your room was a bit neater," she says. "Besides, you already have so many toys."

"I want a toy," insists Tip. "I want the rubber duck!"

"Please don't say 'I want'," his mother tells him.

Tip does convince his mother to let him go on the merry-go-round. But once is not enough!

"Come on Tip, it's time to go. You've gone around five times!" says his mother.

Tip crosses his arms and wrinkles his nose. "One more time! I don't want to get off! I want to try the piglet!"

"An ice cream!" Tip cries as they're walking home. "Buy me a chocolate cone, nice and big!"

"It is not time to eat ice cream, Tip. Soon we will be home and we'll have a nice carrot soup for dinner," Mom replies calmly.

"Tip, do you want to play?" a group of friends call out.
"The ball is mine," Tip replies, holding the ball tightly.
But when his friends go away Tip realizes that playing
alone isn't as much fun.

"Come on, Tip, it is time to go home!" says his mother. "I don't want to walk," whines Tip. "Carry me."

"No, Tip, not now!" says his mother. She is losing her patience. "Walking is good for you and I am tired."

Grrrrr

"I am not coming home! Teddy and I want to stay out!" Tip cries.

"Don't be silly, it will soon be cold, and your father is waiting for us. I still have to make dinner."

"No! No! I am not coming home!" says Tip. He runs away clutching Teddy Bear.

"Tip! Where are you? Come back here right now!" His mother calls, again and again.

Tip stays hidden, and he does not say a word from behind the bush.

Tip's mother finally leaves, but by then it is dark.
Tip comes out of his hiding place.

"How dark it is, and what strange noises there are!
How cold it is! Scary!" thinks Tip. "Mother! Help!
Where are you?" he cries.

Just then his mother comes back, with his father too! By the light of a lantern they spot Tip – he is crying and shaking.

"Here you are! Finally! We were so worried!" his parents say, and they hug him.

"I promise I will behave from now on, and I won't be cranky anymore!" promises Tip. "From now on I'll be a good little mouse. I will clean my room, I won't eat too much candy, and I'll share with my friends. Most of all, I will never run away again!"